Alfred Austin

Soliloquies in Song

Alfred Austin

Soliloquies in Song

ISBN/EAN: 9783744769181

Printed in Europe, USA, Canada, Australia, Japan

Cover: Foto ©Andreas Hilbeck / pixelio.de

More available books at **www.hansebooks.com**

SOLILOQUIES IN SONG

LOQUIES IN SONG

BY

ALFRED AUSTIN

London

MACMILLAN AND CO.

1882

SOME of the pieces in this volume have already appeared in print. Several are published now for the first time.

CONTENTS.

PRELUDE.

I.

WHERE have you been through the long sweet hours
    That follow the fragrant feet of June?
By the banks and the hedgerows gathering flowers,
    Ere the dew of the dawn is sipped by noon.

II.

And sooth each wilding that buds and blows
    You seem to have found and clustered here,
Round the sprays of the rustic child-like rose
    That smiles in one's face till it stirs a tear.

III.

The clambering vetch, and the meadow-sweet tall,
    That nodded good-day as you sauntered past,
And the poppy flaunting atop of the wall,
    As proud as glory, and fades as fast.

IV.

The campion bladders the children burst,
   The bramble that clutches and won't take nay,
And the morning-glory that wakens first
   To the dewy kisses of nursing day.

V.

The prosperous elder that always smells
   Of homely joys and the cares that bless,
And the woodbine's waxen and honeyed cells,
   A hive of the sweetest idleness.

VI.

And this wayside nosegay is all for me,
   For me, the poet—the word sounds strong;—
Well, for him at least, whatever he be,
   Who has loitered his morning away in song.

VII.

And though sweetest poems that ever were writ,
   With the posy that up to my gaze you lift,
Seem void of music and poor of wit,
   Yet I guess your meaning, and take your gift.

VIII.

For 'tis true among fields and woods I sing,
   Aloof from cities, and my poor strains
Were born, like the simple flowers you bring,
   In English meadows and English lanes.

IX.

If e'er in my verse lurks tender thought,
   'Twas borrowed from cushat or blackbird's throat;
If sweetness any, 'twas culled or caught
   From boughs that blossom and clouds that float.

X.

No rare exotics nor forced are these;
   They budded in darkness and throve in storm;
They learned their colour from rain and breeze,
   And from sun and season they took their form.

XI.

They peeped through the drift of the winter snows;
   They waxed and waned with the waning moon;
Their music they stole from the deep-hushed rose,
   And all the year round to them is June.

XII.

So let us exchange, nor ask who gains,
    What each has saved from the morning hours :
Take, such as they are, my wilding strains,
    And I will accept your wilding flowers.

Midsummer 1882.

SOLILOQUIES IN SONG.

BROTHER BENEDICT.

I.

Brother Benedict rose and left his cell
With the last slow swing of the evening bell.
In his hand he carried his only book,
And he followed the path to the Abbey brook,
And, crossing the stepping-stones, paused midway,
For the journeying water seemed to say,

Benedicite.

II.

But when he stood on the other bank,
The flags rose tall, and the grass grew rank,
And the sorrel red and the white meadow-sweet
Shook their dust on his sandalled feet,
And lifting their heads where his girdle hung,
Would surely have said had they found a tongue,

Benedicite.

B

III.

Onward and upward he clomb and wound,

Bruising the thyme on the nibbled ground.

Here and there, in the untrimmed brake,

The dog-rose bloomed for its own sweet sake ;

The woodbine clambered up out of reach,

But the scent of them all breathed as plain as speech,

Benedicite.

IV.

Shortly he came to a leafy nook,

Where wind never entered nor branch ever shook.

Itself was the only thing in sight,

And the rest of the world was shut out quite.

'Twas as self-contained as the holy place

Where the children quire with upturned face,

Benedicite.

V.

A dell so curtained with trunks and boughs,

That in hours when the ringdove coos to his spouse,

The sun to its heart scarce a way could win.

But the trees now had drawn all their shadows in ;

There was nothing but scent in the dewy air,

And the silence seemed saying in mental prayer,

Benedicite.

VI.

'Gainst the trunk of a beech, round, smooth, and gray,

Brother Benedict leaned, with intent to pray,

And opened his book : with vellum bound ;

Within, red letters on faded ground ;

Pater, and Ave, and saving Creed :—

But look where you would, you seemed to read,

Benedicite.

VII.

He scarce had a verse of his office said,

Ere a bird in the branches overhead

Began to warble so sweet a strain,

That strive as he would, still he strove in vain

To close his ears ; so he closed his book,

While the unseen throat to the air outshook

Benedicite.

VIII.

'Twas a song that rippled, and revelled, and ran

Ever back to the note whence it began ;

Rising, and falling, and never did stay,

Like a fountain that feeds on itself all day,

Wanting no answer, answering none,

But beginning again as each verse was done,

Benedicite.

IX.

It brought an ecstasy into his face,
It weaned his senses from time and space,
It carried him off to worlds unseen,
And showed him what is not and ne'er has been,
Transporting his soul to those realms of calm,
More blessèd and blessing than even the psalm,

Benedicite.

X.

Then, carolling still, it drew him thence
Slowly back to the spheres of sense,
But held him awhile where self expires,
And vague recollections and vague desires
Banish the burden of things that are,
And angels seem canticling, faint and far,

Benedicite.

XI.

Then across him there flitted the days that are dead,
And those that will follow when these are fled;
Generations of sorrow, wave after wave,
With their samesome journey from womb to grave;
Men's love of the fleshly sweets that sting,
And the comfort that comes when we kneel and sing,

Benedicite.

XII.

He suddenly started and gazed around,
For silence can waken as well as sound,
And the bird had ceased singing.   The dewy air
Still was immersed in mental prayer.
Time seemed to have stopped.   So he quickened pace,
But forgot not to say ere he left the lone place,

Benedicite.

XIII.

Downward he wended, and under his feet,
As on mounting, the bruised thyme answered sweet;
As before, in the brake the dog-rose bloomed,
And the woodbine with fragrance the hedge perfumed;
And the white meadow-sweet and the sorrel red,
Had they found a tongue, would still surely have said,

Benedicite.

XIV.

But where were the flags and the tall rank grass,
And the stepping-stones smooth for his feet to pass?
Were they swept away?   Did he wake or dream?
A bridge that he knew not spanned the stream;
Though under its archway he still could hear
The journeying water purling clear,

Benedicite.

XV.

Where had he wandered?   This never could
Be the spot where the Abbey orchard stood?
Where the filberts once mellowed, lay tumbled blocks,
And cherry stumps peered through tares and docks;
A rough plot stretched where in times gone by
The plump apples dropped to the joyous cry,

                        Benedicite.

XVI.

The gateway had vanished, the portal flown,
The walls of the Abbey were ivy-grown;
The arches were shattered, the roof was gone
The mullions were mouldering one by one;
Wrecked was the oriel's tracery light
That the sun streamed through when they met to recite

                        Benedicite.

XVII.

Chancel and choir and nave and aisle
Were but one ruinous vacant pile.
So utter the havoc, you could not tell
Which was corridor, cloister, cell.
Cow-grass, and foxglove, and waving weed,
Covered the scrolls where you used to read,

                        Benedicite.

XVIII.

High up where of old the belfry towered,
An elder had rooted and whitely flowered :
Surviving ruin and rain and wind,
Below it a lichened gurgoyle grinned.
Though birds were chirping and flitting about,
They paused not to treble the anthem devout,

Benedicite.

XIX.

Then he went where the Abbot was wont to lay
His children to rest till the Judgment Day,
And at length in the grass the name he found
Of a friar he fancied alive and sound.
The slab was hoary, the carving blurred,
And he rather guessed than could read the word,

Benedicite.

XX.

He sate him down on a fretted stone,
Where rains had beaten and winds had blown,
And opened his office-book, and read
The prayers that we read for our loved ones dead,
While nightfall crept on the twilight air,
And darkened the page of the final prayer,

Benedicite.

XXI.

But to murkiest gloom when the gloaming did wane,
In the air there still floated a shadowy strain.
'Twas distilled with the dew, it was showered from the
    star,
It was murmuring near, it was tingling afar;
In silence it sounded, in darkness it shone,
And in sleep that is deepest it wakeful dreamed on,
                            Benedicite.

XXII.

Do you ask what had witched Brother Benedict's ears?
The bird had been singing a thousand years:
Sweetly confounding in its sweet lay
To-day, to-morrow, and yesterday.
Time?   What is Time but a fiction vain
To him that o'erhears the Eternal strain,
                            Benedicite?

PRIMROSES.

I.

LATEST, earliest of the year,
Primroses that still were here,
Snugly nestling round the boles
Of the cut-down chestnut poles,
When December's tottering tread
Rustled 'mong the deep leaves dead,
And with confident young faces
Peeped from out the sheltered places
When pale January lay
In its cradle day by day,
Dead or living, hard to say,
Now that mid-March blows and blusters,
Out you steal in tufts and clusters,
Making leafless lane and wood
Vernal with your hardihood.
Other lovely things are rare,
You are prodigal as fair.

First you come by ones and ones,
Lastly in battalions,
Skirmish along hedge and bank,
Turn old Winter's wavering flank,
Round his flying footsteps hover,
Seize on hollow, ridge, and cover,
Leave nor slope nor hill unharried,
'Till, his snowy trenches carried,
O'er his sepulchre you laugh,
Winter's joyous epitaph.

II.

This, too, be your glory great,
Primroses, you do not wait,
As the other flowers do,
For the Spring to smile on you,
But with coming are content,
Asking no encouragement.
Ere the hardy crocus cleaves
Sunny borders 'neath the eaves,
Ere the thrush his song rehearse
Sweeter than all poets' verse,
Ere the early bleating lambs
Cling like shadows to their dams,

Ere the blackthorn breaks to white,
Snowy-hooded anchorite ;
Out from every hedge you look,
You are bright by every brook,
Weaving for your sole defence
Fearlessness of innocence.
While the daffodils still waver,
Ere the jonquil gets its savour,
While the linnets yet but pair,
You are fledged, and everywhere.
Nought can daunt you, nought distress,
Neither cold nor sunlessness.
You, when Lent sleet flies apace,
Look the tempest in the face ;
As descend the flakes more slow,
From your eyelids shake the snow,
And when all the clouds have flown,
Meet the sun's smile with your own.
Nothing ever makes you less
Gracious to ungraciousness.
March may bluster up and down,
Pettish April sulk and frown ;
Closer to their skirts you cling,
Coaxing Winter to be Spring.

III.

Then when your sweet task is done,
And the wild-flowers, one by one,
Here, there, everywhere do blow,
Primroses, you haste to go,
Satisfied with what you bring,
Waning morning-star of Spring.
You have brightened doubtful days,
You have sweetened long delays,
Fooling our enchanted reason
To miscalculate the season.
But when doubt and fear are fled,
When the kine leave wintry shed,
And 'mong grasses green and tall
Find their fodder, make their stall;
When the wintering swallow flies
Homeward back from southern skies,
To the dear old cottage thatch
Where it loves to build and hatch,
That its young may understand,
Nor forget, this English land;
When the cuckoo, mocking rover,
Laughs that April loves are over;

When the hawthorn, all ablow,
Mimics the defeated snow;
Then you give one last look round,
Stir the sleepers underground,
Call the campion to awake,
Tell the speedwell courage take,
Bid the eyebright have no fear,
Whisper in the bluebell's ear
Time has come for it to flood
With its blue waves all the wood,
Mind the stitchwort of its pledge
To replace you in the hedge,
Bid the ladysmocks good-bye,
Close your bonnie lids and die;
And, without one look of blame,
Go as gently as you came.

AGATHA.

I.

SHE wanders 'mid the April woods,
　　That glisten with the fallen shower;
She leans her face against the buds,
　　She stops, she stoops, she plucks a flower.
　　She feels the ferment of the hour:
She broodeth when the ringdove broods;
　　The sun and flying clouds have power
Upon her cheek and changing moods.
　　She cannot think she is alone,
　　　　As o'er her senses warmly steal
　　Floods of unrest she fears to own,
　　　　And almost dreads to feel.

II.

Among the summer woodlands wide
　　Anew she roams, no more alone;

The joy she feared is at her side,
  Spring's blushing secret now is known.
  The primrose and its mates have flown,
The thrush's ringing note hath died;
  But glancing eye and glowing tone
Fall on her from her god, her guide.
  She knows not, asks not, what the goal,
    She only feels she moves towards bliss,
  And yields her pure unquestioning soul
    To touch and fondling kiss.

III.

And still she haunts those woodland ways,
  Though all fond fancy finds there now
To mind of spring or summer days,
  Are sodden trunk and songless bough.
  The past sits widowed on her brow:
Homeward she wends with wintry gaze,
  To walls that house a hollow vow,
To hearth where love hath ceased to blaze:
  Watches the clammy twilight wane
    With grief too fixed for woe or tear;
  And with her forehead 'gainst the pane
    Envies the dying year.

LOVE'S BLINDNESS.

Now do I know that Love is blind, for I
Can see no beauty on this beauteous earth,
No life, no light, no hopefulness, no mirth,
Pleasure nor purpose, when thou art not nigh.
Thy absence exiles sunshine from the sky,
Seres Spring's maturity, checks Summer's birth,
Leaves linnet's pipe as sad as plover's cry,
And makes me in abundance find but dearth.
But when thy feet flutter the dark, and thou
With orient eyes dawnest on my distress,
Suddenly sings a bird on every bough,
The heavens expand, the earth grows less and less,
The ground is buoyant as the air, I vow,
And all looks lovely in thy loveliness.

LOVE'S WISDOM.

Now on the summit of Love's topmost peak
Kiss we and part ; no farther can we go :
And better death than we from high to low
Should dwindle or decline from strong to weak.
We have found all, there is no more to seek ;
All have we proved, no more is there to know ;
And Time could only tutor us to eke
Out rapture's warmth with custom's afterglow.
We cannot keep at such a height as this ;
And even straining souls like ours inhale
But once in life so rarefied a bliss.
What if we lingered till love's breath should fail !
Heaven of my Earth ! one more celestial kiss,
Then down by separate pathways to the vale.

c

MY WINTER ROSE.

I.

Why did you come when the trees were bare?
Why did you come with the wintry air?
When the faint note dies in the robin's throat,
And the gables drip and the white flakes float?

II.

What a strange, strange season to choose to come,
When the heavens are blind and the earth is dumb;
When nought is left living to dirge the dead,
And even the snowdrop keeps its bed!

III.

Could you not come when woods are green?
Could you not come when lambs are seen?
When the primrose laughs from its childlike sleep,
And the violets hide and the bluebells peep?

IV.

When the air as your breath is sweet, and skies
Have all but the soul of your limpid eyes,
And the year, growing confident day by day,
Weans lusty June from the breast of May?

V.

Yet had you come then, the lark had lent
In vain his music, the thorn its scent,
In vain the woodbine budded, in vain
The rippling smile of the April rain.

VI.

Your voice would have silenced merle and thrush,
And the rose outbloomed would have blushed to blush,
And Summer, seeing you, paused, and known
That the glow of your beauty outshone its own.

VII.

So, timely you came, and well you chose,
You came when most needed, my winter rose.
From the snow I pluck you, and fondly press
Your leaves 'twixt the leaves of my leaflessness.

A FRAGMENT.

I.

SHOULD fickle hands in far-off days
  No longer stroke thy hair,
And lips that once were proud to praise
  Forget to call thee fair,
Sigh but my name, and though I be
  Mute in the churchyard mould,
I will arise and come to thee,
  And worship as of old.

II.

And should I meet the wrinkled brow,
  Or find the silver tress,
What were't to me, it would be thou,
  I could not love thee less.
'Gainst love time wages bootless strife,
  What now is would be then ;
The cry that brought me back to life
  Would make thee young again.

A WOMAN'S APOLOGY.

In the green darkness of a summer wood,
Wherethro' ran winding ways, a lady stood,
Carved from the air in curving womanhood.

A maiden's form crowned by a matron's mien,
As, about Lammas, wheat-stems may be seen,
The ear all golden, but the stalk still green.

There as she stood, waiting for sight or sound,
Down a dim alley without break or bound,
Slowly he came, his gaze upon the ground.

Nor ever once he lifted up his eyes
Till he no more her presence could disguise;
Then he her face saluted silentwise.

And silentwise no less she turned, as though
She was the leaf and he the current's flow,
And where he went, there she perforce must go.

And both kept speechless as the dumb or dead,
Nor did the earth so much as speak their tread,
So soft by last year's leaves 'twas carpeted.

And not a sound moved all the greenwood through,
Save when some quest with fluttering wings outflew,
Ruffling the leaves ; then silence was anew.

And when the track they followed forked in twain,
They never doubted which one should be ta'en,
But chose as though obeying secret rein.

Until they came where boughs no longer screened
The sky, and soon abruptly intervened
A rustic gate, and over it they leaned.

Leaned over it, and green before them lay
A meadow ribbed with drying swathes of hay,
From which the hinds had lately gone away.

Beyond it, yet more woods, these too at rest,
Smooth-dipping down to shore, unseen, but guessed,
For lo ! the Sea, with nothing on its breast.

I.

"I was sure you would come," she said, with a voice
    like a broken wing
That flutters, and fails, then flags, while it nurses the
    failure's sting;
"You could not refuse me that, 'tis but such a little
    thing.

II.

"Do I remember the words, the farewell words that
    you spoke,
Answering soft with hard, ere we parted under the
    oak?
Remember them? Can I forget? For each of them
    cut like a stroke.

III.

"True—were they true? You think so, or they had
    never been said;
But somehow, like lightning flashes, they flickered
    about my head,
Flickered but touched me not. They ought to have
    stricken me dead.

IV.

"What do I want with you now? What I always
    wanted, you know ;
A voice to be heard in the darkness, a flower to be
    seen in the snow,
And a bond linking each fresh future with the lengthen-
    ing long-ago.

V.

"Is it too much? Too little ! Well, little or much,
    'tis all
That rescues my life from the nothing it seems to be
    when I call
For a life to reply, and my voice comes back like a
    voice from the wall.

VI.

"If one played sweet on a lute, yea so soft that you
    scarce could hear,
Would you clang all the chords with your hand that
    the octaves might ring out clear?
Lo ! asunder the strings are snapped, and the music
    shrinks silent for fear.

VII.

"See! the earth through the infinite spaces goes
  silently round and round,
And the moon moveth on through the heavens and
  never maketh a sound,
And the wheels of eternity traverse their journey in
  stillness profound.

VIII.

"'Tis only the barren breakers that bellow on barren
  shore;
'Tis only the braggart thunders that rumble and rage
  and roar;
Like a wave is the love that babbles; but silent love
  loves evermore.

IX.

"Feeble, shadowy, shallow? Is ocean then shallow
  that keeps
Its harvest of shell and seaweed that none or garners
  or reaps,
That the diver may sound a moment, but never drag
  from its deeps?

X.

"Cowardice? Yes, we are cowards; cowards from
  cradle to bier,
And the terror of life grows upon us as we grow year
  by year;
Our smiles are but trembling ripples urged on by a
  sub-tide of fear.

XI.

"And hence, or at substance or shadow we start,
  though we scarce know why.
Life seems like a haunted wood, where we tremble and
  crouch and cry.
Beast, or robber, or ghost,—our courage is still to fly.

XII.

"So we look around for a guide, and to place all our
  fears in his hand,
That his courage may keep us brave, that his grandeur
  may make us grand:
But, remember, a guide, not an ambush. Oh, tell me
  you understand!

XIII.

"Still silent, still unpersuaded. Ah! I know what
 your thoughts repeat.
We are all alike, and we love to keep passion aglow
 at our feet,
Like one that sitteth in shade and complacently smiles·
 at the heat.

XIV.

"You think so? Then come into shade. Rise up,
 take the seat at my side ;
Or, see, I will kneel, not you. What is humble, if this
 be pride?
What seems cold now will chance feel warm when the
 fierce glare of noon hath died.

XV.

" Have you never, when waves were breaking, watched
 children at sport on the beach,   ✕
With their little feet tempting the foam-fringe, till with
 stronger and further reach
Than they dreamed of, a billow comes bursting, how
 they turn and scamper and screech !

✕ *per, to-day — in Carbis Bay .*
8/7 '96

XVI.

"Are we more than timider children ?   With its blend-
 ing of terror and glee,
To us life—call it love, if you will—is a deep mysteri-
 ous sea,
That we play with till it grows earnest; then straight
 we tremble and flee.

XVII.

"Oh, never the pale east flushes with ripples of rising
 day,
Never, never, the birds awakening sing loud upon
 gable and spray,
But afresh you dawn on my life, and my soul chants
 its matin lay.

XVIII.

"When the scent of the elder is wafted from the hedge
 in the cottage lane,
Up the walk, and over the terrace, and in at the open
 pane,
You are there, and my life seems perfumed like a
 garden after rain.

XIX.

"The nightingale brings you nearer, the woodpecker
    borrows your voice ;
The flower where the bees cling and cluster seems the
    flower of the flowers of your choice.
I am sad with the cloud of your sadness, with the joy
    of your joy I rejoice.

XX.

"What dearer, what nearer would you ?   Once heart
    is betrothed to heart,
No closeness can bring them closer, no parting can
    put them apart.
Oh ! take all the balm, leave the bitter, give the sweet-
    ness with none of its smart."

The blue sea now had saddened into gray ;
Solid and close the darkening woodlands lay,
And twilight's floating dews clung heavy with the hay.

One with all these, he neither stirred nor spake,
Though for a sound the silence seemed to ache,
Waiting and wondering when his voice the pain would
    break.

Then since the words hope forced despair to say
Seemed to have vanished with the vanished day,
She turned her from the gate, and slowly moved away.

And he too turned ; but pacing side by side,
This mocking nearness did them more divide,
Than if betwixt them moaned the round of ocean wide.

But when o'erhead boughs once more met and spanned,
She halted, laid upon his arm her hand,
And questioned blank his face, his heart to understand.

Had trust or tenderness been hovering there,
She would have known it in the duskiest air ;
But face and form alike of every trace was bare.

Her touch he neither welcomed nor repelled ;
Pulses that once had quickened straight seemed
        quelled ;
He stood like one that is by courteous bondage held.

One hand thus foiled, the other rescuing came,
And in the darkness sheltered against shame,
She fawned on him with both, and trembled out his
        name.

Then as a reaper, when the days are meet,
His sickle curves about the bending wheat,
He hollowed out his arms, and harvested his sweet.

XXI.

"Now what shall I cling to?" she murmured, "Be-
    hold! I am weak, you are strong.
Brief, brief is the bridal of summer, the mourning of
    winter is long;
Never leave me unloved to discover love's right was
    but rapturous wrong!"

Again was silence.   Then she slowly felt
The clasp of cruel fondness round her melt,
And heard a voice that seemed the voice of one that
    knelt.

"The long, long mourning of the winter days
Wait sure for them that bask in summer rays;
One must depart, then life is death to one that stays.

"This fixed decree we can nor change nor cheat;
For I must either leave or lose you, sweet,
And all love's triumphs end in death and dark defeat.

"Death is unconscious change, change conscious
    death.
Better to die outright than gasp for breath.
Life, dead, hath done with pain; Love, lingering,
    suffereth.

"The only loss—and this may you be spared !—
For which who stake on love must be prepared,
Is still that, though life may, yet death can not be
    shared.

"No other pain shall come to you from me.
What love withholds, love needs must ask.   But, see !
Since you embrace love's chains, love's self doth set
    you free."

So, free they wandered, drinking with delight
The scented silence of the summer night,
And in the darkness saw what ne'er is seen in light.

Hushed deep in slumber seemed all earthy jars,
And, looking up, they saw, 'twixt leafy bars,
The untrod fields of Heaven glistening with dewy stars.

CONTENT.

WRITTEN OFF ITHACA.

I COULD not find the little maid Content,
So out I rushed, and sought her far and wide ;
But not where Pleasure each new fancy tried,
Heading the maze of reeling merriment,
Nor where, with restless eyes and bow half bent,
Love in a brake of sweetbrier smiled and sighed,
Nor yet where Fame towered crowned and glorified,
Found I her face, nor wheresoe'er I went.
So homeward back I crawled like wounded bird,
When lo ! Content sate spinning at my door :
And when I asked her where she was before—
" Here all the time," she said ; " *I* never stirred ;
Too eager in your search, you passed me o'er,
And, though I called, you neither saw nor heard."

GO AWAY, DEATH!

I.

Go away, Death!
    You have come too soon.
To sunshine and song I but just awaken,
And the dew on my heart is undried and unshaken ;
    Come back at noon.

II.

Go away, Death!
    What a short reprieve !
The mists of the morning have vanished, I roam
Through a world bright with wonder, and feel it my
    home ;
    Come back at eve.

III.

Go away, Death!
        See, it still is light.
Over earth broods a quiet more blissful than glee,
And the beauty of sadness lies low on the sea;
        Come back at night.

IV.

Come to me, Death!
        I no more would stay.
The night-owl hath silenced the linnet and lark,
And the wailing of wisdom sounds sad in the dark;
        Take me away.

LONGING.

I.

The hills slope down to the valley, the streams run
    down to the sea,
And my heart, my heart, O far one! sets and strains
    towards thee.
But only the feet of the mountain are felt by the rim
    of the plain,
And the source and soul of the hurrying stream reach
    not the calling main.

II.

The dawn is sick for the daylight, the morning yearns
    for the noon,
And the twilight sighs for the evening star and the
    rising of the moon.
But the dawn and the daylight never were seen in the
    self-same skies,
And the gloaming dies of its own desire when the
    moon and the stars arise.

III.

The Springtime calls to the Summer, "Oh, mingle your
    life with mine,"
And Summer to Autumn 'plaineth low, "Must the
    harvest be only thine?"
But the nightingale goes when the swallow comes, ere
    the leaf is the blossom fled;
And when Autumn sits on her golden sheaves, then
    the reign of the rose is dead.

IV.

And hunger and thirst, and wail and want, are lost in
    the empty air,
And the heavenly spirit vainly pines for the touch of
    the earthly fair.
And the hills slope down to the valley, the streams
    run down to the sea,
And my heart, my heart, O far one! sets and strains
    towards thee.

IMPROMPTU:

TO FRANCES GARNET WOLSELEY.

LITTLE maiden just beginning
To be comely, arch, and winning,
In whose form I catch the traces
Of your mother's gifts and graces,
And around whose head the glory
Of your father's growing story,
O'er whose cradle, fortune-guided,
Mars and Venus both presided,
May your fuller years inherit
Female charm and manly merit,
So that all may know who girt you
With vivacity and virtue,
Whence you had the luck to borrow
Pensive mien without its sorrow,
Dignity devoid of coldness,
Sprightliness without its boldness,

IMPROMPTU.

Raillery untipped by malice,
Playful wit and kindly sallies,
Eloquence averse from railing,
Each good point without its failing!
And when, little bud, you flower
Into maidenhood and power,
Fate no fainter heart allot you
Than the brave one that begot you,
So that you a race continue
Worthy of the blood within you,
Handing down the gifts you bring them,
With a better bard to sing them.

March 1877.

THE REPLY OF Q. HORATIUS FLACCUS
TO A ROMAN " ROUND-ROBIN."

Good friends, you urge my Odes grow trite,
 And that of worthless station,
Of fleeting youth and joy, I write
 With endless iteration.

But say, in mortals, base or great,
 Have you a change detected ?
Are they, when victors, less elate,
 When vanquished, less dejected?

Do they no more in mundane mire
 For golden garbage scramble ?
Or, but companioned with the lyre,
 Up twisting Anio ramble ?

Hath fortune ceased to prove a jade ?
 Hath favour waxed less fickle ?
Hath shamed Bellona dropped her blade,
 Or Death put up his sickle ?

Doth age no longer rime the hair?
　　Finds Virtue always supper?
Or, when cit. rides a Knight, doth Care
　　No more bestride the crupper?

Do not the rosy hours wax pale,
　　New loves old loves disherit ;
And sleight of golden showers prevail
　　'Gainst Danae's brazen turret?

Sooth, *verbum sap.*   But then, Jove knows!
　　Men are not wise, but foolish,
Whether they scan Soracte's snows,
　　Or those near Ballachulish.

Still, still they hug the bestial sty,
　　And have not changed one wee bit;
Unpleasing truth, which " *Repeti-*
　　Ta decies (non) placebit."

Ask such to share my Sabine meal!
　　To twine the parsley classic!
For such to break the Manlian seal,
　　And liberate my Massic!

A pretty tale !   Why, ken you not,
 Good friends, as lately showed I,
In verse already you've forgot,—
 Profanum vulgus odi?

Fair maid, or Minister, I dine,
 Toast Rome or *Alma Venus:*
When Lydia will not kiss my wine,
 Why, then, I ask Mæcenas.

For such and self the chords I strike
 Of wisdom, love, and scorning ;
And if the world my themes dislike,
 Well,—gentlemen, Good morning !

THREE SONNETS:

WRITTEN IN MID-CHANNEL.

I.

Now upon English soil I soon shall stand,
Homeward from climes that fancy deems more fair ;
And well I know that there will greet me there
No soft foam fawning upon smiling strand,
No scent of orange-groves, no zephyrs bland,
But Amazonian March, with breast half bare
And sleety arrows whistling through the air,
Will be my welcome from that burly land.
Yet he who boasts his birthplace yonder lies,
Owns in his heart a mood akin to scorn
For sensuous slopes that bask 'neath Southern skies,
Teeming with wine and prodigal of corn,
And, gazing through the mist with misty eyes,
Blesses the brave bleak land where he was born.

II.

And wherefore feels he thus?   Because its shore
Nor conqueror's foot nor despot's may defile,
But Freedom walks unarmed about the isle,
And Peace sits cooing beside each man's door.
Beyond these straits, the wild-beast mob may roar,
Elsewhere the veering demagogue beguile :
We, hand in hand with the Past, look on and smile,
And tread the ways our fathers trod before.
What though some wretch, whose glory you may trace
Past lonely hearths and unrecorded graves,
Round his Sword-sceptre summoning swarms of slaves,
Menace *our* shores with conflict or disgrace,—
We laugh behind the bulwark of the waves,
And fling the foam defiant in his face.

III.

And can it be, when Heaven this deep moat made,
And filled it with the ungovernable seas,
Gave us the winds for rampart, waves for frise,
Behind which Freedom, elsewhere if betrayed,
Might shelter find, and flourish unafraid,
That men who learned to lisp at English knees

Of English fame, to pamper womanish ease

And swell the surfeits of voracious trade,

Shall the impregnable breakers undermine,

Take ocean in reverse, and, basely bold,

Burrow beneath the bastions of the brine ?—

Nay, England, if the citadel be sold

For lucre thus, Tarpeia's doom be thine,

And perish smothered in a grave of gold !

March 1882.

A FARMHOUSE DIRGE.

I.

WILL you walk with me to the brow of the hill, to
    visit the farmer's wife,
Whose daughter lies in the churchyard now, eased of
    the ache of life?
Half a mile by the winding lane, another half to the
    top:
There you may lean o'er the gate and rest; she will
    want me awhile to stop,
Stop and talk of her girl that is gone and no more will
    wake or weep,
Or to listen rather, for sorrow loves to babble its pain
    to sleep.

II.

How thick with acorns the ground is strewn, rent from
    their cups and brown!
How the golden leaves of the windless elms come
    singly fluttering down!

The briony hangs in the thinning hedge, as russet as
    harvest corn,
The straggling blackberries glisten jet, the haws are
    red on the thorn;
The clematis smells no more but lifts its gossamer
    weight on high;—
If you only gazed on the year, you would think how
    beautiful 'tis to die.

III.

The stream scarce flows underneath the bridge; they
    have dropped the sluice of the mill;
The roach bask deep in the pool above, and the
    water-wheel is still.
The meal lies quiet on bin and floor; and here where
    the deep banks wind,
The water-mosses nor sway nor bend, so nothing
    seems left behind.
If the wheels of life would but sometimes stop, and
    the grinding awhile would cease,
'Twere so sweet to have, without dying quite, just a
    spell of autumn peace.

IV.

Cottages four, two new, two old, each with its clamber-
    ing rose :
Lath and plaster and weather tiles these, brick faced
    with stone are those.
Two crouch low from the wind and the rain, and tell
    of the humbler days,
Whilst the other pair stand up and stare with a self-
    asserting gaze ;
But I warrant you'd find the old as snug as the new
    did you lift the latch,
For the human heart keeps no whit more warm under
    slate than beneath the thatch.

V.

Tenants of two of them work for me, punctual, sober,
    true ;
I often wish that I did as well the work I have got
    to do.
Think not to pity their lowly lot, nor wish that their
    thoughts soared higher ;
The canker comes on the garden rose, and not on the
    wilding brier.

Doubt and gloom are not theirs and so they but work
    and love, they live
Rich in the only valid boons that life can withhold or
    give.

VI.

Here is the railway bridge, and see how straight do
    the bright lines keep,
With pheasant copses on either side, or pastures of
    quiet sheep.
The big loud city lies far away, far too is the cliff-
    bound shore,
But the trains that travel betwixt them seem as if
    burdened with their roar.
Yet, quickly they pass, and leave no trace, not the
    echo e'en of their noise :
Don't you think that silence and stillness are the
    sweetest of all our joys ?

VII.

Lo ! yonder the Farm, and these the ruts that the
    broad-wheeled wains have worn,
As they bore up the hill the faggots sere, or the mellow
    shocks of corn.

E

The hops are gathered, the twisted bines now brown
    on the brown clods lie,
And nothing of all man sowed to reap is seen betwixt
    earth and sky.
Year after year doth the harvest come, though at
    summer's and beauty's cost :
One can only hope, when our lives grow bare, some
    reap what our hearts have lost.

VIII.

And this is the orchard, small and rude, and uncared-
    for, but oh ! in spring,
How white is the slope with cherry bloom, and the
    nightingales sit and sing !
You would think that the world had grown young once
    more, had forgotten death and fear,
That the nearest thing unto woe on earth was the
    smile of an April tear ;
That goodness and gladness were twin, were one :—
    The robin is chorister now :
The russet fruit on the ground is piled, and the lichen
    cleaves to the bough.

IX.

Will you lean o'er the gate, whilst I go on? You can
    watch the farmyard life,
The beeves, the farmer's hope, and the poults, that
    gladden his thrifty wife;
Or, turning, look on the hazy weald,—you will not be
    seen from here,—
Till your thoughts, like it, grow blurred and vague, and
    mingle the far and near.
Grief is a flood, and not a spring, whatever in grief we
    say;
And perhaps her woe, should she see me alone, will
    run more quickly away.

   .   .   .   .   .

I.

'I thought you would come this morning, ma'am.
    Yes, Edith at last has gone;
To-morrow's a week, ay, just as the sun right into her
    window shone;
Went with the night, the vicar says, where endeth
    never the day;
But she's left a darkness behind her here I wish she
    had taken away.

She is no longer with us, but we seem to be always
 with her,
In the lonely bed where we laid her last, and can't get
 her to speak or stir.

2.

"Yes, I'm at work; 'tis time I was. I should have
 begun before;
But this is the room where she lay so still, ere they
 carried her past the door.
I thought I never could let her go where it seems so
 lonely of nights;
But now I am scrubbing and dusting down, and set-
 ing the place to rights.
All I have kept are the flowers there, the last that
 stood by her bed.
I suppose I must throw them away. *She* looked much
 fairer when she was dead.

3.

"Thank you, for thinking of her so much. Kind
 thought is the truest friend.
I wish you had seen how pleased she was with the
 peaches you used to send.

She tired of *them* too ere the end, so she did with all
    we tried ;
But she liked to look at them all the same, so we set
    them down by her side.
Their bloom and the flush upon her cheek were alike,
    I used to say ;
Both were so smooth, and soft, and round, and both
    have faded away.

4.

" I never could tell you how kind too were the ladies
    up at the hall ;
Every noon, or fair or wet, one of them used to
    call.
Worry and work seems ours, but yours pleasant and
    easy days,
And when all goes smooth, the rich and poor have
    different lives and ways.
Sorrow and death bring men more close, 'tis joy that
    puts us apart ;
'Tis a comfort to think, though we're severed so, we're
    all of us one at heart.

5.

" She never wished to be smart and rich, as so many
    in these days do,
Nor cared to go in on market days to stare at the gay
    and new.
She liked to remain at home and pluck the white
    violets down in the wood ;
She said to her sisters before she died, ' 'Tis so easy
    to be good.'
She must have found it so, I think, and that was the
    reason why
God deemed it needless to leave her here, so took her
    up to the sky.

6.

" The vicar says that he knows she is there, and surely
    she ought to be ;
But though I repeat the words, 'tis hard to believe
    what one does not see.
They did not want me to go to the grave, but I could
    not have kept away,
And whatever I do I can only see a coffin and church-
    yard clay.

Yes, I know it's wrong to keep lingering there, and
 wicked and weak to fret;
And that's why I'm hard at work again, for it helps
 one to forget.

7.

"The young ones don't seem to take to work as their
 mothers and fathers did.
We never were asked if we liked or no, but had to
 obey when bid.
There's Bessie won't swill the dairy now, nor Richard
 call home the cows,
And all of them cry, 'How *can* you, mother?' when
 I carry the wash to the sows.
Edith would drudge, for Death one's hearth of the
 helpful one always robs.
But she was so pretty I could not bear to set her on
 dirty jobs.

8,

"I don't know how it'll be with them when sorrow
 and loss are theirs,
For it isn't likely that they'll escape their pack of
 worrits and cares.

They say it's an age of progress this, and a sight of
    things improves,
But sickness, and age, and bereavement seem to work
    in the same old grooves.
Fine they may grow, and that, but Death as lief takes
    the moth as the grub.
When their dear ones die, I suspect they'll wish they'd
    a floor of their own to scrub.

9.

"Some day they'll have a home of their own, much
    grander than this, no doubt,
But polish the porch as you will you can't keep doctors
    and coffins out.
I've done very well with my fowls this year, but what
    are pullets and eggs,
When the heart in vain at the door of the grave the
    return of the lost one begs?
The rich have leisure to wail and weep, the poor
    haven't time to be sad:
If the cream hadn't been so contrairy this week, I
    think grief would have driven me mad.

10.

"How does my husband bear up, you ask? Well,
    thank you, ma'am, fairly well;
For he too is busy just now, you see, with the wheat
    and the hops to sell:
It's when the work of the day is done, and he comes
    indoors at night,
While the twilight hangs round the window-panes
    before I bring in the light,
And takes down his pipe, and says not a word, but
    watches the faggots roar—
And then I know he is thinking of her who will sit on
    his knee no more.

11.

"Must you be going? It seems so short. But thank
    you for thinking to come;
It does me good to talk of it all, and grief feels
    doubled when dumb.
An the butter's not quite so good this week, if you
    please, ma'am, you must not mind,
And I'll not forget to send the ducks and all the eggs
    we can find;

I've scarcely had time to look round me yet, work gets
 into such arrears,
With only one pair of hands, and those fast wiping
 away one's tears.

12.

" You've got some flowers, yet, haven't you, ma'am ?
 though they now must be going fast ;
We never have any to speak of here, and I placed on
 her coffin the last.
Could you spare me a few for Sunday next ?   I should
 like to go all alone,
And lay them down on the little mound where there
 isn't as yet a stone.
Thank you kindly, I'm sure they'll do, and I promise
 to heed what you say ;
I'll only just go and lay them there, and then I will
 come away."

X.

Come, let us go. Yes, down the hill, and home by
 the winding lane.
The low-lying fields are suffused with haze, as life is
 suffused with pain.

The noon mists gain on the morning sun, so despond-
ency gains on youth;

We grope, and wrangle, and boast, but Death is the
only certain truth.

O love of life! what a foolish love! we should weary
of life did it last.

While it lingers, it is but a little thing; 'tis nothing at
all when past.

XI.

The acorns thicker and thicker lie, the briony limper
grows,

There are mildewing beads on the leafless brier where
once smiled the sweet dog-rose.

You may see the leaves of the primrose push through
the litter of sodden ground;

Their pale stars dream in the wintry womb, and the
pimpernel sleepeth sound.

They will awake; shall *we* awake? Are we more
than imprisoned breath?

When the heart grows weak, then hope grows strong,
but stronger than hope is Death.

THE GOLDEN YEAR!

I.

WHEN piped the love-warm throstle shrill,
　And all the air was laden
With scent of dew and daffodil,
　I saw a youth and maiden,
Whose colour, Spring-like, came and fled,
　'Mong purple copses straying,
While birchen tassels overhead
　Like marriage-bells kept swaying;
Filled with that joy that lingers still,
　Which Eve brought out of Aiden,—
With scent of dew and daffodil
　When all the air was laden.

II.

When primrose banks turn pale and fade,
　And meads wax deep and golden,
And in lush dale and laughing glade
　Summer's gay Court is holden,

Them, nestling close, again I saw,
　　Affianced girl and lover,
She looking up with eyes of awe
　　To burning gaze above her;
Playing anew the part oft played,
　　Sung by the poets olden,—
When primrose banks turn pale and fade,
　　And meads wax deep and golden.

III.

When autumn woods began to glow,
　　And autumn sprays to shiver,
Once more I saw them walking slow,
　　By sedgy-rustling river.
The season's flush was on her cheek,
　　The season's sadness o'er him:
He stroked her hand, and bade her speak
　　Of all the love she bore him.
That only made her tears to flow,
　　And chill his heart to quiver,—
While autumn woods began to glow,
　　And autumn sprays to shiver.

IV.

When winter's fields stretched stiff and stark,
   And wintry winds shrilled eerie,
I saw him creep, alone, at dark,
   Into the churchyard dreary.
He laid him down against the stone,
   'Neath which she aye lay sleeping,
Kissed its cold face with many a moan,
   Then loudly fell a-weeping :
"Oh ! let me in from lonely cark,
   Or come thou back, my dearie !"—
But the wintry fields stretched stiff and stark,
   And the wintry winds shrilled eerie !

SONG.

I.

Go talk to her, sweet flower,
    To whom I fain would talk ;
Tell her I hour by hour
    Pine on my own poor stalk.

II.

Tell her that I should live
    Not quite so sore distressed,
If she to you would give
    A throne upon her breast.

III.

Tell her that should she hie
    To my parched plot to see
If I be dead, that I
    No more should withered be.

IV.

If I were dead, her feet
  My spirit would revive,
As may her bosom sweet
  Keep you, sweet flower, alive.

FELIX OPPORTUNITATE MORTIS.

EXILE or Cæsar?   Death hath solved thy doubt,
And made thee certain of thy changeless fate ;
And thou no more hast wearily to wait,
Straining to catch the people's tarrying shout
That from unrestful rest would drag thee out,
And push thee to those pinnacles of State
Round which throng courtly loves, uncourted hate,
Servility's applause, and envy's flout.

x   Twice happy boy ! though cut off in thy flower,
The timeliest doom of all thy race is thine :
Saved from the sad alternative, to pine
For heights unreached, or icily to tower,
Like Alpine crests that only specious shine,
And glitter on the lonely peak of Power.

June 1879.

x   *The Prince Imperial.*

F

UNSEASONABLE SNOWS.

THE leaves have not yet gone ; then why do ye come,
O white flakes falling from a dusky cloud ?
But yesterday my garden-plot was proud
With uncut sheaves of ripe chrysanthemum.
Some trees the winds have stripped ; but look on some,
'Neath double load of snow and foliage bowed,
Unnatural winter fashioning a shroud
For Autumn's burial ere its pulse be numb.
Yet Nature plays not an inhuman part :
In her, our own, vicissitudes we trace.
Do we not cling to our accustomed place,
Though journeying Death have beckoned us to start ?
And faded smiles oft linger in the face,
While grief's first flakes fall silent on the heart !

October 1880.

A SPRING CAROL.

I.

BLITHE friend! blithe throstle! Is it thou,
    Whom I at last again hear sing,
Perched on thy old accustomed bough,
    Poet-prophet of the Spring?
Yes! Singing as thou oft hast sung,
I can see thee there among
The clustered branches of my leafless oak;
    Where, thy plumage gray as it,
    Thou mightst unsuspected sit,
    Didst thou not thyself betray
    With thy penetrating lay, .
Swelling thy mottled breast at each triumphant stroke
    Wherefore warble half concealed,
    When thy notes are shaft and shieid,
    And no hand that lives would slay
    Singer of such a roundelay?

Telling of thy presence thus,

Be nor coy nor timorous!

   Sing loud !   Sing long !

   And let thy song

Usurp the air 'twixt earth and sky :

   Let it soar and sink and rally,

   Ripple low along the valley,

Break against the fir-trees high,

   Ofttimes pausing, never dying,

   While we lean where fancy bids,

   Listening, with half-closèd lids,

Unto the self-same chant, most sweet, most satisfying.

II.

Where hast thou been all the dumb winter days,

When neither sunlight was nor smile of flowers,

   Neither life, nor love, nor frolic,

   Only expanse melancholic,

With never a note of thy exhilarating lays ?

   But, instead, the raven's croak,

   Sluggish dawns and draggled hours,

   Gusts morose and callous showers,

   Underneath whose cutting stroke

Huddle the seasoned kine, and even the robin cowers.

Wast curled asleep in some snug hollow
    Of my hybernating oak,
Through the dripping weeks that follow
    One another slow, and soak
Summer's extinguished fire and autumn's drifting
        smoke?
    Did its waking awake thee,
    Or thou it with melody?
    Or together did ye both
    Start from winter's sleep and sloth,
And the self-same sap that woke
    Bole and branch, and sets them budding,
    Is thy throat with rapture flooding?
    Or, avoiding icy yoke,
When golden leaves floated on silver meres,
And pensive Autumn, keeping back her tears,
    Nursed waning Summer in her quiet lap,
    Didst thou timely pinions flap,
    Fleeing from a land of loss,
    And, with happy mates, across
Ocean's restless ridges travel,
    To that lemon-scented shore
        Where, beneath a deep-domed sky,
        Carven of lapis-lazuli,

Golden sunlight evermore

Glistens against golden gravel,

Nor ever a snowflake falls, nor rain-clouds wheel and

ravel ;

Clime where I wandered once among

Ruins old with feelings young,

Whither too I count to fly

When my songful seasons die,

And with the self-same spell which, first when

mine,

Intensified my youth, to temper my decline.

III.

Wherefore dost thou sing, and sing ?

Is it for sheer joy of singing ?

Is it to hasten lagging Spring,

Or greet the Lenten lilies through turf and tuft up-

springing ?

Dost thou sing to earth or sky ?

Never comes but one reply :

Carol faint, carol high,

Ringing, ringing, ringing !

Are those iterated trills

For the down-looking daffodils,

That have strained and split their sheath,
And are listening underneath?
Or but music's prompting note,
Whereunto the lambs may skip?
Haply dost thou swell thy throat,
Only to show thy craftsmanship?
Wouldst thou pipe if none should hearken?
If the sky should droop and darken,
And, as came the hills more close,
Moody March to wooing Spring
Sudden turned a mouth morose,—
Unheeded wouldst, unheeding, sing?
What is it rules thy singing season?
Instinct, that diviner reason,
To which the thirst to know seemeth a sort of
treason?
If it be,
Enough for me,
And any motive for thy music I
Will not ask thee to impart,
Letting my head play traitor to my heart,
Too deeply questioning why.
Sing for nothing, if thou wilt,
Or, if thou for aught must sing,

Sing unto thy anxious spouse,
Sitting somewhere 'mong the boughs,
In the nest that thou hast built,
Underneath her close-furled wing
Future carols fostering.
Sing, because it is thy bent;
Sing, to heighten thy content!
Sing, for secret none can guess;
Sing for very uselessness!
Sing for love of love and pleasure,
Unborn joy, unfound treasure,
Rapture no words can reach, yearning no thoughts
    can measure!

IV.

Why dost thou ever cease to sing?
    Singing is such sweet comfort, who,
    If he could sing the whole year through,
    Would barter it for anything?
Why do not thou and joy their reign assert
Over winter, death, and hurt?
If thou forcest them to flee,
They in turn will banish thee,

Making life betwixt ye thus
Mutably monotonous.
O, why dost thou not perch and pipe perpetually ?
All the answer I do get,
Is louder, madder music yet ;
Thus rebuking : Thou dost err !
I am no philosopher ;
Only a poet, forced to sing,
When the cold gusts gather and go,
When the earth stirs in its tomb,
And, asudden, witching Spring
Into her bosom sucks the snow,
To give it back in thorn and cherry-
bloom.
When along the hedgerows twinkle
Roguish eyes of periwinkle,
When with undulating glee
Yaffles scream from tree to tree,
And on every bank are seen
Primroses that long have been
Lying in wait with ambushed eyes
To break forth when Winter flies,
Joined by all things swift and sweet,
Following him with noiseless feet,

Pelting him with April showers,
Chasing and chanting his defeat,
Till with undisputed flowers
Thronged are all the lanes to greet
Dove-like inspiring Spring, many-voiced Paraclete.

V.

Therefore, glad bird ! warble, and shrill, and carol,
Now that Earth whom winter stripped,
Putteth on her Spring apparel,
Daintily woven, gaily tipped ;
Now that in the tussocked mead
Lambkins one another jostle,—
Carol, carol ! jocund throstle !
Impregnating the air with thy melodious seed,
Which, albeit scattered late,
Now will quickly germinate,
Giving us who waited long
Vernal harvest of ripe song.
Which, I do perceive, was sent
Nowise to deepen argument,
Rather to teach me how, like thee,
To merge doubt in melody.

Sing, sing away,

All through the day,

Lengthening out the twilight gray,

And with thy trebles of delight

Invade the threshold of the night :

Until felicity, too high, too deep,

Saturated senses steep,

And all that lives and loves subside to songless sleep.

ALL HAIL TO THE CZAR!

I.

ALL hail to the Czar! By the fringe of the foam
That thunders, untamed, around Albion's shore,
See multitudes throng, dense as sea-birds whose home
Is betwixt the deaf rocks and the ocean's mad roar;
And across the ridged waters stand straining their eyes
For a glimpse of the Eagle that comes from afar:
Lo! it swoops towards the beach, and they greet it
     with cries
That silence the billows—" All hail to the Czar!"

II.

All hail to the Czar! England's noblest and best,
Her oldest, her newest, her proudest are there,
And they vie in obeisance before the great guest,
For the prize of his nod, for the alms of his stare.

To the seat of their Empire they draw him along,
Where the Palace flies open to welcome his car,
And Prince, Press, and People, with leader and song,
Ring the change on the pæan—"All hail to the Czar!"

III.

All hail to the Czar! the bold Monarch who shook
From the heart of the Lion its insolent lust,
That once from the strongest no outrage would brook,
Till it crouched at his feet, till it crawled in the dust!
Who the laurels bequeathed to us tore from our brow,
Who extinguished our fame that once shone like a star,
Made our rulers to tremble, our heralds to bow,
And our bosoms to mock us—"All hail to the Czar!"

IV.

All hail to the Czar! O yes! show him your ships,
Had your courage not failed, he had seen before now,
As they dally at anchor, the gag on their lips,
And the peace-loving holiday trim on their prow!
Yes! show him your army, that mighty array
He so rashly defied when he ventured to mar
The last work of its hands, and remind it to say,
But with bayonets inverted—"All hail to the Czar!"

V.

All hail to the Czar !   As ye revel and feast,
I marvel the ghosts of the bootlessly slain
Do not come from their cold lonely graves in the East,
From the hillside that looks o'er the desolate main,
Which they perished to save, ye surrender, to live,
To the man ye now slaver, all base as ye are !
Do not stalk through the banquet-hall, pallid, and give
The gay toast ere ye drink it—" All hail to the Czar !"

VI.

All hail to the Czar !   For his daughter he gave,
Like Atrides of old, without shrinking or qualm,
Though not that the white ships might move o'er the
         wave,
But that ours still might ride in immovable calm !
What Religion could once, now can Statecraft persuade;
And if ye would devote to the furies of war
Half as freely your sons as he gave up his maid,
Without shame might ye shout then—" All hail to the
         Czar !"

VII.

All hail to the Czar!   Are ye then sunk so low,
O ye sons of the once fearless masters of earth !
That ye pour out the wine for an insolent foe,
That in depths of dishonour ye simulate mirth?
That, like unto mongrel hounds beaten and cowed,
Ye, crouched, lick alternately smiter and scar?—
Oh, rather my country lay deaf in its shroud,
Than had lived to hear silent—"All hail to the Czar!"

May 1874.

AT HIS GRAVE.

I.

LEAVE me a little while alone,
Here at his grave that still is strewn
    With crumbling flower and wreath ;
The laughing rivulet leaps and falls,
The thrush exults, the cuckoo calls,
    And he lies hushed beneath.

II.

With myrtle cross and crown of rose,
And every lowlier flower that blows,
    His new-made couch is dressed :
Primrose and cowslip, hyacinth wild,
Gathered by Monarch, peasant, child,
    A nation's grief attest.

III.

I stood not with the mournful crowd
That hither came when round his shroud
    Pious farewells were said.
In the famed city that he saved,
By minaret crowned, by billow laved,
    I heard that he was dead.

IV.

Now o'er his tomb at last I bend,
No greeting get, no greeting tend,
    Who never came before
Unto his presence, but I took,
From word or gesture, tone or look,
    Some wisdom from his door.

V.

And must I now unanswered wait,
And, though a suppliant at the gate,
    No sound my ears rejoice?
Listen! Yes, even as I stand,
I feel the pressure of his hand,
    The comfort of his voice.

G

VI.

How poor were Fame, did grief confess
That death can make a great life less,
    Or end the help it gave !
Our wreaths may fade, our flowers may wane,
But his well-ripened deeds remain,
    Untouched, above his grave.

VII.

Let this, too, soothe our widowed minds ;
Silenced are the opprobrious winds
    Whene'er the sun goes down ;
And free henceforth from noonday noise,
He at a tranquil height enjoys
    The starlight of renown.

VIII.

Thus hence we something more may take
Than sterile grief, than formless ache,
    Or vainly-uttered vow ;
Death hath bestowed what life withheld,
And he round whom detraction swelled,
    Hath peace with honour now.

IX.

The open jeer, the covert taunt,
The falsehood coined in factious haunt,
    These loving gifts reprove.
They never were but thwarted sound
Of ebbing waves that bluster round
    A rock that will not move.

X.

And now the idle roar rolls off,
Hushed is the gibe and shamed the scoff,
    Repressed the envious gird ;
Since death, the looking-glass of life,
Cleared of the misty breath of strife,
    Reflects his face unblurred.

XI.

From callow youth to mellow age,
Men turn the leaf and scan the page,
    And note, with smart of loss,
How wit to wisdom did mature,
How duty burned ambition pure,
    And purged away the dross.

XII.

Youth is self-love ; our manhood lends
Its heart to pleasure, mistress, friends,
    So that when age steals nigh,
How few find any worthier aim
Than to protract a flickering flame,
    Whose oil hath long run dry !

XIII.

But he, unwitting youth once flown,
With England's greatness linked his own,
    And steadfast to that part,
Held praise and blame but fitful sound,
And in the love of country found
    Full solace for his heart.

XIV.

Now in an English grave he lies :
With flowers that tell of English skies
    And mind of English air,
A grateful Sovereign decks his bed,
And hither long with pilgrim tread
    Will the English race repair.

XV.

Yet not beside his grave alone
We seek the glance, the touch, the tone;
    His home is nigh,—but there,
See from the hearth his figure fled,
The pen unraised, the page unread,
    Untenanted the chair!

XVI.

Vainly the beechen boughs have made
A fresh green canopy of shade,
    Vainly the peacocks stray;
While Carlo, with despondent gait
Wonders how long affairs of State
    Will keep his lord away.

XVII.

Here most we miss the guide, the friend.
Back to the churchyard let me wend,
    And, by the posied mound,
Lingering where late stood worthier feet,
Wish that some voice, more strong, more sweet,
    A loftier dirge would sound.

XVIII.

At least I bring not tardy flowers,
Votive to him life's budding powers,
　　Such as they were, I gave—
He not rejecting : so I may
Perhaps these poor faint spices lay,
　　Unchidden, on his grave !

HUGHENDEN, *May* 12, 1881.

THE DEATH OF HUSS.

In the streets of Constance was heard the shout,
"Masters! bring the arch-heretic out!"
The stake had been planted, the faggots spread,
And the tongues of the torches flickered red.
"Huss to the flames!" they fiercely cried:
Then the gates of the Convent opened wide.

Into the sun from the dark he came,
His face as fixed as a face in a frame.
His arms were pinioned, but you could see,
By the smile round his mouth, that his soul was free;
And his eye with a strange bright glow was lit,
Like a star just before the dawn quencheth it.

To the pyre the crowd a pathway made,
And he walked along it with no man's aid;
Steadily on to the place he trod,
Commending aloud his soul to God.

Aloud he prayed, though they mocked his prayer :
He was the only thing tranquil there.

But, seeing the faggots, he quickened pace,
As we do when we see the loved one's face.
" Now, now, let the torch in the resin flare,
Till my books and body be ashes and air !
But the spirit of both shall return to men,
As dew that rises descends again."

From the back of the crowd where the women wept,
And the children whispered, a peasant stepped.
A goodly faggot was on his back,
Brittle and sere, from last year's stack ;
And he placed it carefully where the torch
Was sure to lick and the flame to scorch.

" Why bring you fresh fuel, friend ?   Here are sticks
To burn up a score of heretics ?"
Answered the peasant, " Because this year,
My hearth will be cold, for is firewood dear ;
And Heaven be witness I pay my toll,
And burn your body to save my soul."

Huss gazed at the peasant, he gazed at the pile,
Then over his features there stole a smile.
" *O Sancta Simplicitas !* By God's troth,
This faggot of yours may save us both,
And He who judgeth perchance prefer
To the victim the executioner !"

Then unto the stake was he tightly tied,
And the torches were lowered and thrust inside.
You could hear the twigs crackle and sputter the flesh,
Then " *Sancta Simplicitas !*" moaned afresh.
'Twas the last men heard of the words he spoke,
Ere to Heaven his soul went up with the smoke.

A NIGHT IN JUNE.

I.

LADY ! in this night of June,
  Fair like thee and holy,
Art thou gazing at the moon
  That is rising slowly ?
    I am gazing on her now :
    Something tells me, so art thou.

II.

Night hath been when thou and I
  Side by side were sitting,
Watching o'er the moonlit sky
  Fleecy cloudlets flitting.
    Close our hands were linkèd then ;
    When will they be linked again ?

III.

What to me the starlight still,
　　Or the moonbeams'. splendour,
If I do not feel the thrill
　　Of thy fingers slender?
　　　　Summer nights in vain are clear,
　　　　If thy footstep be not near.

IV.

Roses slumbering in their sheaths
　　O'er my threshold clamber,
And the honeysuckle wreathes
　　Its translucent amber
　　　　Round the gables of my home :
　　　　How is it thou dost not come?

V.

If thou camest, rose on rose
　　From its sleep would waken ;
From each flower and leaf that blows
　　Spices would be shaken ;
　　　　Floating down from star and tree,
　　　　Dreamy perfumes welcome thee.

VI.

I would lead thee where the leaves
 In the moon-rays glisten ;
And, where shadows fall in sheaves,
 We would lean and listen
  For the song of that sweet bird
  That in April nights is heard.

VII.

And when weary lids would close,
 And thy head was drooping,
Then, like dew that steeps the rose,
 O'er thy languor stooping,
  I would, till I woke a sigh,
  Kiss thy sweet lips silently.

VIII.

I would give thee all I own,
 All thou hast would borrow
I from thee would keep alone
 Fear and doubt and sorrow.
  All of tender that is mine,
  Should most tenderly be thine.

IX.

Moonlight! into other skies,
   I beseech thee wander.
Cruel, thus to mock mine eyes,
   Idle, thus to squander
      Love's own light on this dark spot;—
      For my lady cometh not!

AT VAUCLUSE.

I.

By Avignon's dismantled walls,
Where cloudless mid-March sunshine falls,
   Rhone, through broad belts of green,
Flecked with the light of almond groves,
Upon itself reverting, roves
   Reluctant from the scene.

II.

Yet from stern moat and storied tower,
From sprouting vine, from spreading flower,
   My footsteps cannot choose
But turn aside, as though some friend
Were waiting for my voice, and wend
   Unto thy vale, Vaucluse!

III.

For here, by Sorgue's sequestered stream,
Did Petrarch fly from fame, and dream
   Life's noonday light away;
Here build himself a studious home,
And, careless of the crowns of Rome,
   To Laura lend his lay:

IV.

Teaching vain tongues that would reward
With noisy praise the shrinking bard,
   Reminding thus the proud,
Love's sympathy, to him that sings,
Is more than smiles of courts and kings,
   Or plaudits of the crowd.

V.

For poor though love that doth not rouse
To deeds of glory dreaming brows,
   What but a bitter sweet
Is loftiest fame, unless it lay
The soldier's sword, the poet's bay,
   Low at some loved one's feet?

VI.

Where are his books? His garden, where?
I mount from flowery stair to stair,
 While fancy fondly feigns
Here stood his learned lintel, here
He wooed the seasons of the year,
 Here mellowed he his strains.

VII.

On trackless slopes and brambled mounds
The laurel still so thick abounds,
 That Nature's self, one deems,
Regretful of his vanished halls,
Still plants the tree whose name recalls
 The lady of his dreams.

VIII.

Aught more than this I cannot trace.
There is no footstep, form, nor face
 To vivify the scene;
Save where, but culled to fling away,
Posies of withering wildflowers say,
 "Here children's feet have been."

IX.

Yet there's strange softness in the skies :
The violet opens limpid eyes,
    The woodbine tendrils start ;
Like childhood, winning without guile,
The primrose wears a constant smile,
    And captive takes the heart.

X.

All things remind of him, of her.
Stripped are the slopes of beech and fir,
    Bare rise the crags above ;
But hillside, valley, stream, and plain,
The freshness of his muse retain,
    The fragrance of his love.

XI.

Why did he hither turn ?   Why choose
Thy solitary gorge, Vaucluse ?
    Thy Fountain makes reply,
That, like the muse, its waters well
From source none ne'er can sound, and swell
    From springs that run not dry.

XII.

Or was it he might drink the air
That Laura breathed in surging prayer
    Or duty's stifled sigh ;
Feel on his cheek the self-same gale,
And listen to the same sweet wail
    When summer nights are nigh ?

XIII.

May-be. Of Fame he deeply quaffed :
But thirsting for the sweeter draught
    Of Love, alas for him !
Though draining glory to the dregs,
He was like one that vainly begs,
    And scarcely sips the brim.

XIV.

Is it then so, that glory ne'er
Its throne with happiness will share,
    But, baffling half our aim,
Grief is the forfeit greatness pays,
Lone places grow the greenest bays,
    And anguish suckles fame ?

XV.

Let this to lowlier bards atone,
Whose unknown Laura is their own,
    Possessing and possest ;
Of whom if sooth they do not sing,
'Tis that near her they fold their wing,
    To drop within her nest.

XVI.

Adieu, Vaucluse !   Swift Sorgue, farewell !
Thy winding waters seem to swell
    Louder as I depart ;
But evermore, where'er I go,
Thy stream will down my memory flow,
    And murmur through my heart.

GEORGE ELIOT.

DEAD! Is she dead?
And all that light extinguished!
Mend your words,
Those gropings of the blind along plain paths
Where all the Heavens are shining! Know you not,
Though the Eternal Luminary dips
Below our cramped horizon, leaving here
Only a train of glory, he but goes
To dawn on other and neglected worlds,
Benighted of his presence! So with her,
Whose round imagination, like the sun,
Drew the sad mists of the low-lying earth
Up to her own great altitude, and there
Made them in smiling tears evaporate.
Announce the sun's self dead, and o'er him roll
An epitaph of darkness;—then aver
She too has set for ever.

> Think it thus,
If for sweet comfort's sake.   What we call death
Is but another sentinel despatched
To relieve life, weary of being on guard,
Whose active service is not ended here,
But after intermission is renewed
In other fields of duty.   This to her
Was an uncertain promise, since it seems,
Unto the eye of seriousness, unreal,
That, like a child, death should but play with life,
Blowing it out, to blow it in again.
This contradiction over, now she stands
Certain of all uncertainty, and dwells
Where death the sophist puzzles life no more,
But with disdainful silence or clear proof
Confuted is for ever.

> Yet our loss
By others' gain is mended not, and we
Sit in the darkness that her light hath left.
Comfort our grief with symbols as we will,
Her empty throne stares stony in our face,
And with a dumb relentlessness proclaims
That she has gone for ever, for ever gone,
Returning not. . . . How plain I see her now,

The twilight tresses, deepening into night,
The brow a benediction, and the eyes
Seat where compassion never set, and like
That firm, fixed star, which altereth not its place
While all the planets round it sink and swim,
Shone with a steady guidance.   O, and a voice
Matched with whose modulations softest notes
Of dulcimer by daintiest fingers stroked,
Or zephyrs wafted over summer seas,
On summer shores subsiding, sounded harsh.
Listening whereto, steeled obduracy felt
The need to kneel, necessity to weep,
And craving to be comforted ; a shrine
Of music and of incense and of flowers,
Where hearts, at length self-challenged, were content
Still to be sad and sinful, so they might
Feel that exonerating pity steal
In subtle absolution on their guilt.
                    Dead?   Never dead !
That this, man's insignificant domain,
Which is not boundary of space, should be
The boundary of life, revolts the mind,
Even when bounded.   Into soaring space
Soar, spacious spirit ! unembarrassed now

By earthly boundaries, and circle up
Into the Heaven of Heavens, and take thy place
Where the Eternal Morning broadens out
To recognise thy coming.   Realm on Realm
Of changeless revolution round thee roll,
Thou moving with them, and among the stars
Shine thou a star long looked for ; or, unbuoyed
Beyond the constellations of our ken,
Traverse the infinite azure with thy heart,
And with love's light elucidate the Spheres ;
While we, below, this meek libation pour,
Mingled of honey and hyssop, on thy grave !

December 29, 1880.

THE LAST REDOUBT.

I.

Kacelyevo's slope still felt
The cannon's bolt and the rifles' pelt;
For a last redoubt up the hill remained,
By the Russ yet held, by the Turk not gained.

II.

Mehemet Ali stroked his beard;
His lips were clinched and his look was weird;
Round him were ranks of his ragged folk,
Their faces blackened with blood and smoke.

III.

"Clear me the Muscovite out!" he cried.
Then the name of "Allah!" echoed wide,
And the rifles were clutched and the bayonets lowered,
And on to the last redoubt they poured.

IV.

One fell, and a second quickly stopped
The gap that he left when he reeled and dropped;
The second,—a third straight filled his place;
The third,—and a fourth kept up the race.

V.

Many a fez in the mud was crushed,
Many a throat that cheered was hushed,
Many a heart that sought the crest
Found Allah's throne and a houri's breast.

VI.

Over their corpses the living sprang,
And the ridge with their musket-rattle rang,
Till the faces that lined the last redoubt
Could see their faces and hear their shout.

VII.

In the redoubt a fair form towered,
That cheered up the brave and chid the coward;
Brandishing blade with a gallant air,
His head erect and his bosom bare.

VIII.

" Fly ! they are on us !" his men implored ;
But he waved them on with his waving sword.
"It cannot be held; 'tis no shame to go !"
But he stood with his face set hard to the foe.

IX.

Then clung they about him, and tugged, and knelt.
He drew a pistol from out his belt,
And fired it blank at the first that set
Foot on the edge of the parapet.

X.

Over, that first one toppled ; but on
Clambered the rest till their bayonets shone,
As hurriedly fled his men dismayed,
Not a bayonet's length from the length of his blade.

XI.

" Yield !"   But aloft his steel he flashed,
And down on their steel it ringing clashed ;
Then back he reeled with a bladeless hilt,
His honour full, but his life-blood spilt.

XII.

Mehemet Ali came and saw
The riddled breast and the tender jaw.
" Make her a bier of your arms," he said,
" And daintily bury this dainty dead ! "

XIII.

They lifted him up from the dabbled ground ;
His limbs were shapely, and soft, and round.
No down on his lip, on his cheek no shade :—
" Bismillah !" they cried, " 'tis an Infidel maid !"

XIV.

" Dig her a grave where she stood and fell,
'Gainst the jackal's scratch and the vulture's smell.
Did the Muscovite men like their maidens fight,
In their lines we had scarcely supped to-night."

XV.

So a deeper trench 'mong the trenches there
Was dug, for the form as brave as fair ;
And none, till the Judgment trump and shout,
Shall drive her out of the Last Redoubt.

GRANDMOTHER'S TEACHING.

I.

"GRANDMOTHER dear, you do not know; you have
    lived the old-world life,
Under the twittering eaves of home, sheltered from
    storm and strife;
Rocking cradles, and covering jams, knitting socks for
    baby feet,
Or piecing together lavender bags for keeping the
    linen sweet:
Daughter, wife, and mother in turn, and each with a
    blameless breast,
Then saying your prayers when the nightfall came, and
    quietly dropping to rest.

II.

"You must not think, Granny, I speak in scorn, for
    yours have been well-spent days,

And none ever paced with more faithful feet the
dutiful ancient ways.

Grandfather's gone, but while he lived you clung to
him close and true,

And mother's heart, like her eyes, I know, came to
her straight from you.

If the good old times, at the good old pace, in the
good old grooves would run,

One could not do better, I'm sure of that, than do as
you all have done.

III.

" But the world has wondrously changed, Granny, since
the days when you were young ;

It thinks quite different thoughts from then, and
speaks with a different tongue.

The fences are broken, the cords are snapped, that
tethered man's heart to home ;

He ranges free as the wind or the wave, and changes
his shore like the foam.

He drives his furrows through fallow seas, he reaps
what the breakers sow,

And the flash of his iron flail is seen mid the barns of
the barren snow.

IV.

" He has lassoed the lightning and led it home, he has
    yoked it unto his need,
And made it answer the rein and trudge as straight as
    the steer or steed.
He has bridled the torrents and made them tame, he
    has bitted the champing tide,
It toils as his drudge and turns the wheels that spin for
    his use and pride.
He handles the planets and weighs their dust, he
    mounts on the comet's car,
And he lifts the veil of the sun, and stares in the eyes
    of the uttermost star.

V.

" 'Tis not the same world you knew, Granny; its
    fetters have fallen off;
The lowliest now may rise and rule where the proud
    used to sit and scoff.
No need to boast of a scutcheoned stock, claim rights
    from an ancient wrong;
All are born with a silver spoon in their mouths whose
    gums are sound and strong.

And I mean to be rich and great, Granny; I mean it
    with heart and soul :
At my feet is the ball, I will roll it on, till it spins
    through the golden goal.

VI.

"Out on the thought that my copious life should
    trickle through trivial days,
Myself but a lonelier sort of beast, watching the cattle
    graze,
Scanning the year's monotonous change, gaping at
    wind and rain,
Or hanging with meek solicitous eyes on the whims of
    a creaking vane ;
Wretched if ewes drop single lambs, blest so is oilcake
    cheap,
And growing old in a tedious round of worry, surfeit,
    and sleep.

VII.

"You dear old Granny, how sweet your smile, and how
    soft your silvery hair !
But all has moved on while you sate still in your cap
    and easy-chair.

The torch of knowledge is lit for all, it flashes from
    hand to hand;
The alien tongues of the earth converse, and whisper
    from strand to strand.
The very churches are changed and boast new hymns,
    new rites, new truth;
Men worship a wiser and greater God than the half-
    known God of your youth.

VIII.

"What! marry Connie and set up house, and dwell
    where my fathers dwelt,
Giving the homely feasts they gave and kneeling where
    they knelt?
She is pretty, and good, and void I am sure of vanity,
    greed, or guile;
But she has not travelled nor seen the world, and is
    lacking in air and style.
Women now are as wise and strong as men, and vie
    with men in renown;
The wife that will help to build my fame was not bred
    near a country town.

IX.

" What a notion! to figure at parish boards, and wrangle
  o'er cess and rate,

I, who mean to sit for the county yet, and vote on an
  Empire's fate;

To take the chair at the Farmers' Feast, and tickle
  their bumpkin ears,

Who must shake a senate before I die, and waken a
  people's cheers!

In the olden days was no choice, so sons to the roof
  of their fathers clave:

But now! 'twere to perish before one's time, and to
  sleep in a living grave.

X.

"I see that you do not understand.   How should
  you?   Your memory clings

To the simple music of silenced days and the skirts of
  vanishing things.

Your fancy wanders round ruined haunts, and dwells
  upon oft-told tales;

Your eyes discern not the widening dawn, nor your
  ears catch the rising gales.

I

But live on, Granny, till I come back, and then perhaps
you will own

The dear old Past is an empty nest, and the Present
the brood that is flown."

I.

" AND so, my dear, you've come back at last ?   I always
fancied you would.

Well, you see the old home of your childhood's days
is standing where it stood.

The roses still clamber from porch to roof, the elder is
white at the gate,

And over the long smooth gravel path the peacock
still struts in state.

On the gabled lodge, as of old, in the sun, the pigeons
sit and coo,

And our hearts, my dear, are no whit more changed,
but have kept still warm for you.

II.

" You'll find little altered, unless it be me, and that
since my last attack ;

But so that you only give me time, I can walk to the
church and back.

You bade me not die till you returned, and so you see
I lived on:

I'm glad that I did now you've really come, but it's
almost time I was gone.

I suppose that there isn't room for us all, and the old
should depart the first.

That's as it should be.   What is sad, is to bury the
dead you've nursed.

III.

" Won't you have bit nor sup, my dear?   Not even a
glass of whey?

The dappled Alderney calved last week, and the
baking is fresh to-day.

Have you lost your appetite too in town, or is it you've
grown over-nice?

If you'd rather have biscuits and cowslip wine, they'll
bring them up in a trice.

But what am I saying?   Your coming down has set
me all in a maze:

I forgot that you travelled here by train; I was thinking of coaching days.

IV.

" There, sit you down, and give me your hand, and tell
    me about it all,

From the day that you left us, keen to go, to the pride
    that had a fall.

And all went well at the first ?   So it does, when we're
    young and puffed with hope ;

But the foot of the hill is quicker reached the easier
    seems the slope.

And men thronged round you, and women too !   Yes,
    that I can understand.

When there's gold in the palm, the greedy world is
    eager to grasp the hand.

V.

" I heard them tell of your smart town house, but I
    always shook my head.

One doesn't grow rich in a year and a day, in the time
    of my youth 'twas said.

Men do not reap in the spring, my dear, nor are
    granaries filled in May,

Save it be with the harvest of former years, stored up
    for a rainy day.

The seasons will keep their own true time, you can
    hurry nor furrow nor sod :
It's honest labour and steadfast thrift that alone are
    blest by God.

VI.

"You say you were honest. I trust you were, nor do
    I judge you, my dear :
I have old-fashioned ways, and it's quite enough to
    keep one's own conscience clear.
But still the commandment, "Thou shalt not steal,"
    though a simple and ancient rule,
Was not made for modern cunning to baulk, nor for
    any new age to befool ;
And if my growing rich unto others brought but penury,
    chill, and grief,
I should feel, though I never had filched with my
    hands, I was only a craftier thief.

VII.

"That isn't the way they look at it there? All wor-
    shipped the rising sun ?
Most of all the fine lady, in pride of purse you fancied
    your heart had won.

I don't want to hear of her beauty or birth : I reckon
 her foul and low ;
Far better a steadfast cottage wench than grand loves
 that come and go.
To cleave to their husbands, through weal, through
 woe, is all women have to do :
In growing as clever as men they seem to have matched
 them in fickleness too.

VIII.

" But there's one in whose heart has your image still
 dwelt through many an absent day,
As the scent of a flower will haunt a closed room,
 though the flower be taken away.
Connie's not quite so young as she was, no doubt, but
 faithfulness never grows old ;
And were beauty the only fuel of love, the warmest
 hearth soon would grow cold.
Once you thought that she had not travelled, and
 knew neither the world nor life :
Not to roam, but to deem her own hearth the whole
 world, that's what a man wants in a wife.

IX.

" I'm sure you'd be happy with Connie, at least if your
    own heart's in the right place.
She will bring you nor power, nor station, nor wealth,
    but she never will bring you disgrace.
They say that the moon, though she moves round the
    earth, never turns to him morning or night
But one face of her sphere, and it must be because
    she's so true a satellite ;
And Connie, if into your orbit once drawn by the
    sacrament sanctioned above,
Would revolve round you constantly, only to show the
    one-sided aspect of love.

X.

" You will never grow rich by the land, I own ; but if
    Connie and you should wed,
It will feed your children and household too, as it you
    and your fathers fed.
The seasons have been unkindly of late ; there's a
    wonderful cut of hay,
But the showers have washed all the goodness out, till
    it's scarcely worth carting away.

There's a fairish promise of barley straw, but the ears
    look rusty and slim :
I suppose God intends to remind us thus that some-
    thing depends on Him.

XI.

" God neither progresses nor changes, dear, as I once
    heard you rashly say :
Man's schools and philosophies come and go, but His
    word doth not pass away.
We worship Him here as we did of old, with simple
    and reverent rite :
In the morning we pray Him to bless our work, to
    forgive our transgressions at night.
To keep His commandments, to fear His name, and
    what should be done, to do,—
That's the beginning of wisdom still ; I suspect 'tis the
    end of it too.

XII.

" You must see the new-fangled machines at work, that
    harrow, and thresh, and reap ;
They're wonderful quick, there's no mistake, and they
    say in the end they're cheap.

But they make such a clatter, and seem to bring the
rule of the town to the fields:
There's something more precious in country life than
the balance of wealth it yields.
But that seems going; I'm sure I hope that I shall be
gone before:
Better poor sweet silence of rural toil than the factory's
opulent roar.

XIII.

"They're a mighty saving of labour, though; so at
least I hear them tell,
Making fewer hands and fewer mouths, but fewer
hearts as well:
They sweep up so close that there's nothing left for
widows and bairns to glean;
If machines are growing like men, man seems to be
growing a half machine.
There's no friendliness left; the only tie is the wage
upon Saturday nights:
Right used to mean duty; you'll find that now there's
no duty, but only rights.

XIV.

"Still stick to your duty, my dear, and then things
cannot go much amiss.

What made folks happy in bygone times, will make
    them happy in this.
There's little that's called amusement, here ; but why
    should the old joys pall?
Has the blackbird ceased to sing loud in spring? Has
    the cuckoo forgotten to call?
Are bleating voices no longer heard when the cherry-
    blossoms swarm?
And have home, and children, and fireside lost one
    gleam of their ancient charm?

XV.

"Come, let us go round ; to the farmyard first, with its
    litter of fresh-strewn straw,
Past the ash-tree dell, round whose branching tops the
    young rooks wheel and caw ;
Through the ten-acre mead that was mown the first,
    and looks well for aftermath,
Then round by the beans—I shall tire by then,—and
    home up the garden-path,
Where the peonies hang their blushing heads, where
    the larkspur laughs from its stalk—
With my stick and your arm I can manage. But see !
    There, Connie comes up the walk."

TO ENGLAND.

MEN deemed thee fallen, did they? fallen like Rome,
Coiled into self to foil a Vandal throng :
Not wholly shorn of strength, but vainly strong ;
Weaned from thy fame by a too happy home,
Scanning the ridges of thy teeming loam,
Counting thy flocks, humming thy harvest song,
Callous, because thyself secure, 'gainst wrong,
Behind the impassable fences of the foam !
The dupes ! Thou dost but stand erect, and lo !
The nations cluster round ; and while the horde
Of wolfish backs slouch homeward to their snow,
Thou, 'mid thy sheaves in peaceful seasons stored,
Towerest supreme, victor without a blow,
Smilingly leaning on thy undrawn sword !

April 1878.

POETS' CORNER.

I.

I STAND within the Abbey walls,
Where soft the slanting sunlight falls
    In gleams of mellow grace :
The organ swells, the anthem soars,
And waves of prayerful music pours
    Throughout the solemn space.

II.

Slowly the chanted yearning dies :
Then spoken supplications rise,
    Upfloating to the sky ;
The organ peals anew, again
Is silent, and there linger then
    Only my soul and I.

III.

But what are these mute busts that gaze
On me from out the vanished days,
    And bid me pause and scan
Tablet, inscription, title, date,
All that records the vain estate
    Of transitory man?

IV.

Read I aright? And can it be,
Old Abbey, that dead bards in thee
    A resting-place have found?
Is not this consecrated air?
This is the house, the home, of prayer,
    This, this is sacred ground.

V.

And who were they? Their fretful life
With heavenly precept was at strife;
    No pious peace they knew:
Like thunderstorms, against the wind
They pressed, and from their lurid mind
    Alarming lightnings flew.

VI.

Creeds were to them but chains to break ;
No formulas their thirst could slake,
    No faith their hunger feed ;
Their prayers were breathed to unscaled crags,
They worshipped where the eagle flags,
    And the snow-streams flash and speed.

VII.

Their temple was the earth, the air,
The stars that in night's silence share ;
    Unto the plunging brine
Listening, they heard a sacred hymn,
And deep within the woodlands dim
    Found transept, aisle, and shrine.

VIII.

All shapes of sensuous beauty stole
A pathway to the poet's soul ;
    An unresisting slave
To smiles that win, to tears that melt,
Whatever hearts can feel, he felt,
    Whatever ask for, gave.

IX.

His heart to love as quick he lent,
As flower to wandering wind its scent,
　　Or lark to sun its song;
He spent himself in gusts of joy,
Chased the fair phantoms that decoy,
　　And youth's brief reign prolong.

X.

Yet it was wise as well as just
Not upon his rebellious dust
　　The Abbey gates to close,
But bid him hither wend, and find,
What life refused his eager mind,
　　Glory and yet repose.

XI.

For should there come that threatened day,
When creeds shall fade, when faith decay,
　　And worship shall have ceased,
Then, when all formal guides shall fail,
Mankind will in the Poet hail
　　A prophet and a priest.

XII.

He will instruct us still to strain
Towards something to redress our pain,
    To elevate our joy ;
Something responding to that sense
Of restlessness that calls us hence,
    And makes existence cloy.

XIII.

What though commandment, dogma, rite,
One after one, shall perish quite,
    The Poet still will keep
The Sanctuary's lamp alight,
And, in the body's deepest night,
    Forbid the soul to sleep.

XIV.

Then, apprehended right, his lays
Shall seem a hymn of prayer and praise
    To purify from stain ;
Shall bridge with love the severed years,
Instil the sacredness of tears,
    The piety of pain.

XV.

Devotion at his touch shall wake,
The fountains of emotion quake
      With tenderness divine ;
His melody our cravings lift
Upward, and have the saving gift
      Of sacramental wine.

XVI.

Let him then rest where now he lies,
So that if narrower ritual dies,
      Devout feet still may come,
Confessing, what his strains impart,
The deep religion of the heart,
      That never will be dumb.

K

NIGHTINGALE AND CUCKOO.

O NIGHTINGALE and cuckoo ! it was meet
That you should come together ; for ye twain
Are emblems of the rapture and the pain
That in the April of our life compete,
Until we know not which is the more sweet,
Nor yet have learned that both of them are vain !
Yet why, O nightingale ! break off thy strain,
While yet the cuckoo doth his call repeat ?
Not so with me.   To sweet woe did I cling
Long after echoing happiness was dead,
And so found solace.   Now, alas ! the sting !
Cuckoo and nightingale alike have fled ;
Neither for joy nor sorrow do I sing,
And autumn silence gathers in their stead.

A SLEEPLESS NIGHT

WITHIN the hollow silence of the night
I lay awake and listened. I could hear
Planet with punctual planet chiming clear,
And unto star star cadencing aright.
Nor these alone : cloistered from deafening sight,
All things that are, made music to my ear :
Hushed woods, dumb caves, and many a soundless
    mere,
With Arctic mains in rigid sleep locked tight.
But ever with this chant from shore and sea,
From singing constellation, humming thought,
And life through time's stops blowing variously,
A melancholy undertone was wrought ;
And from its boundless prison-house I caught
The awful wail of lone Eternity.

CELESTIAL HEIGHTS.

I.

HAIL! steep ascents and winding ways,
Glimmering through melting morning haze,
  Hail! mountain herd-bells chiming clear!
Hail! meads and cherry-orchards green,
And hail, thrice hail! thou golden mean,
  The châlet's simple cheer!

II.

I leave the highwayed world behind,
And amid pathless pinewoods wind,
  I drink their aromatic air;
Leap with kin feet the leaping stream,
And wake, as from an evil dream,
  To dawn and speechless prayer.

III.

Louder I hear the cattle-bells,
Wider the prospect spreads and swells,
    Lakes, mountains, snow-peaks, round me throng;
I veil mine eyes, with awe oppressed,
Then gaze, and with a carolling breast
    Burst into native song.

IV.

The moist cool dews are round my feet;
Forests of wild-flowers, simple, sweet,
    With honey load each vacant breeze,
Which healing bears upon its wing,
Breathes with an air of more than Spring,
    And banishes disease.

V.

My limbs their youthful stride regain,
From off me fall fatigue and pain,
    I mount more borne on wings than feet;
My blood in faster current flows,
Yet like stream fed by mountain snows,
    Is coolest when most fleet.

VI.

And not this common frame alone
Reclaims its youth, remounts its throne ;
    I feel, as air and sky expand,
That here the spirit, as the flesh,
Grows fragrant, dewy, healthful, fresh,
    And like the landscape, grand !

VII.

Is it then so ?   And must the soul,
That unseen wing towards unseen goal,
    Disdain the crowded vale's delights,
Its heat unfruitful, vapid noise,
And soaring, solitary, poise
    Among celestial heights ?

VIII.

Even so.   And, poised aloft, my soul
Far above human fret and dole
    In empyrean calm abides.
No mortal voice the silence mars ;
I hear the singing of the stars,
    And the eternal tides.

IX.

The greedy aims, the lean regrets,
The disenchantment Hope begets
    On ravished hearts,—beheld from here,
Like unto hamlet, pasture, stream,
Confused in one indifferent dream,
    Mean and minute appear.

X.

Man's feeble fury, trivial hate,
The pains that upon pleasure wait,
    The exhaustion of tumultuous love,
The hopes that dwindle, fears that grow,
All that upheaves the plain below,
    Tranquil, I breathe above.

XI.

Yet 'mid these sun-confronting peaks,
The undesisting spirit seeks
    To mount to loftier, rarer height.
Are what we see but toys of sense,
And we who see them but a lens
    Refracting heavenly light?—

XII

—Imperfect mirror, faulty glass,
Who let the pure white rays to pass
 But twist the coloured beams awry
Belittle all the good we see,
And ill, since of our own degree
 Absorb, to magnify?

XIII.

Who knoweth, or shall answer find?
I hear the rising of the wind,
 More near and full the torrent's plash;
The swaying pine-woods murmur deep,
The lightnings laugh, and, roused from sleep,
 The storm-winds meet and crash!

XIV.

From underneath their lurid cowls,
Rossberg 'gainst Rigi frowns and scowls,
 Across Arth's vale that cowers for dread;
And, mustering for their awful goal,
The phalanxed thunders, rumbling, roll
 Around Pilatus' head!

XV.

Zug's gentle bosom heaves with fear,
And Küssnacht's waves, late soft and clear
    As maiden's gaze or childhood's kiss,
Wax black as murkiest pool of hell
When the infernal tempests swell,
    And demons jeer and hiss.

XVI.

'Mid such a ferment what is Man ?
He sits beneath the rainbow's span,
    And contemplates his little state :
He hears the darkness call, and deems
The skies speak to him in his dreams,
    And recognise him great.

XVII.

Yet is't for him the Heavens engage
In their reverberating rage,
    For him the ambushed levins fight ?
Him ?—but a fainter lightning-flash,
Him ?—but a feebler thunder-crash,
    Ending in deeper night !

XVIII.

Lo ! unto other lands of air
The elemental furies bear
　　The roar of unexhausted strife ;
And, freed from the sepulchral gloom,
Earth once again, as from the tomb,
　　Rises to light and life.

XIX.

Pilatus frees his rugged head,
Zug's crouching lake, released from dread,
　　Looks up and smiles with face serene ;
And, gazed on by the dying sun,
The phantom snow-crests, one by one,
　　Glow with transfigured mien.

XX.

Dead ! And the tender twilight sighs.
Wan wane her cheeks, moist grow her eyes,
　　She draws her robes of mourning round :
Slowly she lights her widowed lamp,
And listens, through the night-dews damp,
　　To catch some cheering sound.

XXI.

Yet in her loneliness how fair !
There is a sadness in the air
    Sweeter than all the chords of joy ;
A fragrance, as of spices borne
Unto the tomb of one we mourn,
    And can no more annoy !

XXII.

Cham's spire, I scarce in heaven descry,
Inverted, in that other sky,
    The lake's lit breast, still plain doth glow :
So Soul, that darkly points above,
Shows sure and clear, when glassed by love
    In answering heart below !

XXIII.

No more the grazing herds I see,
But still their bells chime silvery
    The tuneful, if unmeasured peal,
And, as when heard in dewy morn,
From lonely mind and heart forlorn
    Their desolation steal.

XXIV.

The legions of the starry host,
Each to their high and solemn post
        In silent discipline repair,
And, from the unbattlemented sky,
With an intrepid calm defy
        The demons of the air.

XXV.

And, lo ! athwart their ordered lines,
That strange auxiliary shines,
        Who wears the bright long-flowing crest ;
Weird warrior from another world,
Whose banner shortly will be furled,
        Or waved in realms unguessed.

XXVI.

Erratic pilgrim ! go not yet !
And, each fair planet, do not set !
        For once, if only once, O Time !
Stay thine interminable march
Round and still round that hollow arch,
        Where æons vainly chime !

XXVII.

For when the tide, which unto Heaven
Brings night, 'gainst earth is backward driven
    In waves of rising day, ah ! then
Me helpless will it bear once more
Unto that thronged but barren shore,
    Ploughed by the cares of men !

FELSENEGG.

SHELLEY'S DEATH.

["A little while ago, there died at Spezzia an old sailor, who in his last confession to the priest (whom he told to make it public) stated that he was one of the crew that ran down the boat containing Shelley and Williams, which was done under the impression that the rich Milord Byron was on board with lots of money.   They did not intend to sink the boat, but to board her and murder Byron."—*Letter to Mr. Trelawny from his Daughter, published in the " Times" of Wednesday, December* 1, 1875.]

WHAT !   And it *was* so !   Thou wert then
  Death-stricken from behind,
O heart of hearts ! and they were men,
  That rent thee from mankind !
   Greedy hatred chasing love,
   As a hawk pursues a dove,
Till the soft feathers float upon the careless wind.

  Loathed life ! that I might break the chain
   Which links my kind with me,
  To think that human hands for gain
   Should have been turned 'gainst *thee,*—

Thee that wouldst have given thine all
For the poor, the sick, the thrall,
And weighed thyself as dross, 'gainst their felicity !

We deemed that Nature, jealous grown,
Withdrew the glimpse she gave,
In thy bright genius, of her own,
And, not to slay, but save,
That she timely took back thus
What had been but lent to us,
Shrouding thee in her winds, and lulling 'neath her wave.

For it seemed meet thou shouldst not long
Toss on life's fitful billow,
Nor sleep 'mid mounds of silenced wrong
Under the clay-cold willow :
Rather that thou shouldst recline
Amid waters crystalline,
The sea-shells at thy feet, and sea-weed for thy pillow.

We felt we had no right to keep
What never had been ours ;
That thou belongedst to the deep,
And the uncounted hours ;

That thou earthly no more wert
Than the rainbow's melting skirt,
The sunset's fading bloom, and midnight's shooting
showers.

And, thus resigned, our empty hands
Surrendered thee to thine,
Thinking thee drawn by kindred bands
Under the swirling brine,
Playing there on new-strung shell,
Tuned to Ocean's mystic swell,
Thy lyrical complaints and rhapsodies divine.

But now to hear no sea-nymph fair
Submerged thee with her smile,
And tempests were content to spare
Thee to us yet awhile,
But for ghouls in human mould
Ravaging the seas for gold,—
Oh! this blots out the heavens, and makes mere living
vile!

Yet thy brief life presaged such death,
And it was meet that they

Who poisoned, should have quenched, thy breath,
   Who slandered thee, should slay ;
     That thy spirit, long the mark
     Of the dagger drawn in dark,
Should by the ruffian's stroke be ravished from the
   day.

Hush ! From the grave where I so oft
   Have stood, 'mid ruined Rome,
   I seem to hear a whisper soft
     Wafted across the foam ;
     Bidding justest wrath be still,
     Good feel lovingly for ill,
As exiles for rough paths that help them to their
   home.

OFF MESOLONGI.

I.

THE lights of Mesolongi gleam
    Before me, now the day is gone ;
And vague as leaf on drifting stream,
    My keel glides on.

II.

No mellow moon, no stars arise ;
    In other lands they shine and roam :
All I discern are darkening skies
    And whitening foam.

III.

So on those lights I gaze that seem
    Ghosts of the beacons of my youth,
Ere, rescued from their treacherous gleam,
    I steered towards truth.

IV.

And you, too, Byron, did awake,
　　And ransomed from the cheating breath
Of living adulation, stake
　　Greatness on death !

V.

Alas ! the choice was made too late.
　　You treated Fame as one that begs,
And having drained the joys that sate
　　Offered the dregs.

VI.

The lees of life you scornful brought,
　　Scornful she poured upon the ground :
The honoured doom in shame you sought,
　　You never found.

VII.

· " The Spartan borne upon his shield "
　　Is not the meed of jaded lust ;
And ere your feet could reach the field,
　　Death claimed your dust.

VIII.

Upon the pillow, not the rock,
　　Like meaner things you ebbed away,
Yearning in vain for instant shock
　　Of mortal fray.

IX.

The futile prayer, the feeble tear,
　　All that deforms the face of death,
You had to bear, whilst in your ear
　　Hummed battle's breath.

X.

You begged the vulture, not the worm,
　　Might feed upon your empty corse.
In vain !　Just Nemesis was firm
　　'Gainst late remorse.

XI.

Too much you asked, too little gave,
　　The crown without the cross of strife.
What is it earns a soldier's grave ?
　　A soldier's life.

XII.

Think not I come to taunt the dead.
　　My earliest master still is dear;
And what few tears I have to shed,
　　Are gathering here.

XIII.

Behind me lies Ulysses' isle,
　　The wanderer wise who pined for home.
But Byron! Neither tear nor smile
　　Forbade you roam.

XIV.

Yours was that bitterest mortal fate,
　　No choice save thirst or swinish trough:
Love's self but offered sensuous bait,
　　Or virtuous scoff.

XV.

Yet was it well to wince, and cry
　　For anguish, and at wrong to gird?
Best,—like your gladiator, die
　　Without a word!

XVI.

There be, who in that fault rejoice,
    Since sobs survive as sweetest lays,
And yours remains the strongest voice
    Of later days.

XVII.

For me, I think of you as One
    Who vaguely pined for worthier lot
Than to be blinked at like the sun,
    But found it not.

XVIII.

Who blindly fought his way from birth,
    Nor learned, till 'twas too late to heed,
Not all the noblest songs are worth
    One noble deed :

XIX.

Who, with the doom of glory cursed,
    Still played the athlete's hollow part,
And 'neath his bay-green temples nursed
    A withered heart.

xx.

On, silent keel, through silent sea,
    I will not land where He, alas !
Just missed Fame's crown.   Enough for me
    To gaze, and pass.

April 1881.

AVE MARIA.

I.

In the ages of Faith, before the day
When men were too proud to weep or pray,
There stood in a red-roofed Breton town
Snugly nestled 'twixt sea and down,
A chapel for simple souls to meet,
Nightly, and sing with voices sweet,

Ave Maria !

II.

There was an idiot, palsied, bleared,
With unkempt locks and a matted beard,
Hunched from the cradle, vacant-eyed,
And whose head kept rolling from side to side ;
Yet who, when the sunset-glow grew dim,
Joined with the rest in the twilight hymn,

Ave Maria !

III.

But when they up-got and wended home,
Those up the hillside, these to the foam,
He hobbled along in the narrowing dusk,
Like a thing that is only hull and husk;
On as he hobbled, chanting still,
Now to himself, now loud and shrill,

Ave Maria!

IV.

When morning smiled on the smiling deep,
And the fisherman woke from dreamless sleep,
And ran up his sail, and trimmed his craft,
While his little ones leaped on the sand and laughed,
The senseless cripple would stand and stare,
Then suddenly holloa his wonted prayer,

Ave Maria!

V.

Others might plough, and reap, and sow,
Delve in the sunshine, spin in snow,
Make sweet love in a shelter sweet,
Or trundle their dead in a winding-sheet;
But he, through rapture, and pain, and wrong,
Kept singing his one monotonous song,

Ave Maria!

VI.

When thunder growled from the ravelled wrack,
And ocean to welkin bellowed back,
And the lightning sprang from its cloudy sheath,
And tore through the forest with jaggèd teeth,
Then leaped and laughed o'er the havoc wreaked,
The idiot clapped with his hands, and shrieked,

Ave Maria !

VII.

Children mocked, and mimicked his feet,
As he slouched or sidled along the street ;
Maidens shrank as he passed them by,
And mothers with child eschewed his eye ;
And half in pity, half scorn, the folk
Christened him, from the words he spoke,

Ave Maria.

VIII.

One year when the harvest feasts were done,
And the mending of tattered nets begun,
And the kittiwake's scream took a weirder key
From the wailing wind and the moaning sea,
He was found, at morn, on the fresh-strewn snow,
Frozen, and faint, and crooning low,

Ave Maria !

IX.

They stirred up the ashes between the dogs,
And warmed his limbs by the blazing logs,
Chafed his puckered and bloodless skin,
And strove to quiet his chattering chin;
But, ebbing with unreturning tide,
He kept on murmuring till he died,

Ave Maria!

X.

Idiot, soulless, brute from birth,
He could not be buried in sacred earth;
So they laid him afar, apart, alone,
Without or a cross, or turf, or stone,
Senseless clay unto senseless clay,
To which none ever came nigh to say,

Ave Maria!

XI.

When the meads grew saffron, the hawthorn white,
And the lark bore his music out of sight,
And the swallow outraced the racing wave,
Up from the lonely, outcast grave
Sprouted a lily, straight and high,
Such as She bears to whom men cry,

Ave Maria!

XII.

None had planted it, no one knew
How it had come there, why it grew ;
Grew up strong, till its stately stem
Was crowned with a snow-white diadem,—
One pure lily, round which, behold !
Was written by God in veins of gold,

"Ave Maria !"

XIII.

Over the lily they built a shrine,
Where are mingled the mystic bread and wine ;
Shrine you may see in the little town
That is snugly nestled 'twixt deep and down.
Through the Breton land it hath wondrous fame,
And it bears the unshriven idiot's name,

Ave Maria.

XIV.

Hunchbacked, gibbering, blear-eyed, halt,
From forehead to footstep one foul fault,
Crazy, contorted, mindless-born,
The gentle's pity, the cruel's scorn,
Who shall bar you the gates of Day,
So you have simple faith to say,

Ave Maria ?

SWEET LOVE IS DEAD.

SWEET Love is dead:
  Where shall we bury him?
In a green bed,
With no stone at his head,
  And no tears nor prayers to worry him.

Do you think he will sleep,
  Dreamless and quiet?
Yes, if we keep
Silence, nor weep
  O'er the grave where the ground-worms riot.

By his tomb let us part.
  But hush! he is waking!
He hath winged a dart,
And the mock-cold heart
  With the woe of want is aching.

Feign we no more
   Sweet Love lies breathless.
All we forswore
Be as before ;
   Death may die, but Love is deathless.

THE END.

Printed by R. & R. CLARK, *Edinburgh.*

www.ingramcontent.com/pod-product-compliance
Lightning Source LLC
Chambersburg PA
CBHW020007030726
47500CB00002B/481